# FROGGY GOES TO SCHOOL

# FROGGY GOES TO SCHOOL

by JONATHAN LONDON
illustrated by FRANK REMKIEWICZ

**PUFFIN BOOKS**

This one is for the teachers—
their patience, patience, patience.
—J. L.


For Sarah and the Roadrunners
—F. R.

PUFFIN BOOKS
Published by the Penguin Group
Penguin Putnam Books for Young Readers, 345 Hudson Street, New York, New York 10014, U.S.A.
Penguin Books Ltd, 27 Wrights Lane, London W8 5TZ, England
Penguin Books Australia Ltd, Ringwood, Victoria, Australia
Penguin Books Canada Ltd, 10 Alcorn Avenue, Toronto, Ontario, Canada M4V 3B2
Penguin Books (N.Z.) Ltd, 182-190 Wairau Road, Auckland 10, New Zealand

Penguin Books Ltd, Registered Offices: Harmondsworth, Middlesex, England

First published in the United States of America by Viking, a division of Penguin Books USA Inc., 1996
Published by Puffin Books, a member of Penguin Putnam Books for Young Readers, 1998

10 9

Text copyright © Jonathan London, 1996
Illustrations copyright © Frank Remkiewicz, 1996
All rights reserved

THE LIBRARY OF CONGRESS HAS CATALOGED THE VIKING EDITION AS FOLLOWS:
London, Jonathan.
Froggy goes to school / by Jonathan London ; illustrated by Frank Remkiewicz.  p.  cm.
Summary: Froggy is nervous about his first day of school, but, even though it's hard to sit still, he has a wonderful time.
ISBN 0-670-86726-8 (hc)  [1. First day of school—Fiction. 2. Schools—Fiction. 3. Frogs—Fiction.] I. Remkiewicz, Frank, ill. II. Title.
PZ7.L8432Frg 1996 [E]—dc20 95-53751 CIP AC

Puffin Books ISBN 0-14-056247-8

Printed in the United States of America

It was the first day of school.
Froggy woke up
and looked out the window.
The sun was high in the sky.
"Oh no! The bus! The bus!" he cried.
"I'll miss the bus!"

He hopped out of bed

and flopped outside—*flop flop flop*.

The school bus was leaving.
"Wait! Wait!" he yelled,
and took a mighty hop.

The bus hissed to a stop
and the door folded open.
Froggy flopped up the steps—*flop flop flop*—
but when he reached the top
everybody laughed
and pointed their fingers.

"Wha-a-a-a-t?"
"Did you forget something?"
Froggy looked down.
"Oops!" He was in his *underwear!*

He dashed to the back of the bus and hid behind Max's umbrella all the way to school.

At school, he hopped behind bushes.

He tried to hide behind the flagpole.

He rolled down the hall
like a bowling ball.

And in class, he pretended
to be a flowerpot.

Froggy rubbed his eyes.
He had been dreaming.
He was still in bed!
"Rise and shine, Froggy," said his father.
"It's the first day of school!"

This time Froggy got *all* dressed—
*zip! zoop! zup!*
*zut! zut! zut! zat!*
Then he flopped into the kitchen—
*flop flop flop.*

He tried to pour milk on his bowl of flies,
but the carton flew out of his hands.
"You're just nervous about school, Froggy,"
said his mother. "*Everybody* is, the first day."
"Not me!" cried Froggy.

And together they leapfrogged
all the way to the bus stop—*flop flop flop*.

At school, Froggy found
his name tag on his table.

He liked his name.
It was the first word
he knew how to read.

It was the only word
he knew how to read.

He read it aloud, louder and louder.

cried his teacher, Miss Witherspoon.

"Wha-a-a-a-at?"
"Hush, dear. It's time to pay attention."

But it was hard to pay attention.
He squirmed.

He looked out the window
at the falling leaves.
He felt like a leaf,
falling . . . falling . . .

*PLOP!* He fell out of his chair. "Oops!"
"Kindly stay in your seat, dear,"
said Miss Witherspoon.
"We'll sit on the floor at circle time."

At circle time, Miss Witherspoon said,
"Now children, today I'd like you to tell us
what you did last summer.
Who wants to go first?"
Froggy shouted, "Me me me me me!"
and so did Max.
Miss Witherspoon went
*clap    clap    clap clap clap*—
and everybody went
*clap    clap    clap clap clap* with her.
Then they grew very quiet.
"Now one at a time,"
said Miss Witherspoon.

When Froggy's turn came,
he jumped up and said,
"Last summer, I learned how to swim!"
And he sang, "Bubble bubble, toot toot.
Chicken, airplane, soldier."

Everybody jumped up and joined in—
"Bubble bubble, toot toot.
Chicken, airplane, soldier"—

when—*uh-oh*—in walked the principal, Mr. Mugwort.
"Bubble bubble—*oops!*" cried Froggy,
looking more red in the face than green.
Mr. Mugwort glared at him . . .

then he joined in—
"Bubble bubble, toot toot.
Chicken, airplane, soldier"—
till the bell rang for recess.

When Froggy flopped off the bus after school,
his father said, "Froggy!
How was your first day of school?"
"Great!" said Froggy.
"I taught the principal how to swim!"

"Hmmmmm, that's nice," said his mother,
"but where's your lunch box and baseball cap?"
"Oops! I left them at school."
"Oh, Froggy. Will you ever *learn*?" said his mother.
"That's why I'm going to *school,* Mom!"
And together they leapfrogged

all the way home—*flop flop flop.*

E
Lon

London, Jonathan,
1947-

Froggy goes to
school.

| DATE | | | |
|---|---|---|---|
| | | | |
| | | | |
| | | | |
| | | | |
| | | | |
| | | | |
| | | | |
| | | | |
| | | | |
| | | | |
| | | | |
| | | | |
| | | | |